Granmama's and Vincent's Dreamland Journey

Book 6

Vincent's
Dream Freeze
Ice Cream Parlor

Written and Illustrated by Diana Hastings

This is a work of fiction. All of the characters, names, incidents, organizations, and dialogue in this novel are either the products of the author's imagination or are used fictitiously.

WestBow Press books may be ordered through booksellers or by contacting:

WestBow Press
A Division of Thomas Nelson & Zondervan
1663 Liberty Drive
Bloomington, IN 47403
www.westbowpress.com
844-714-3454

Because of the dynamic nature of the Internet, any web addresses or links contained in this book may have changed since publication and may no longer be valid. The views expressed in this work are solely those of the author and do not necessarily reflect the views of the publisher, and the publisher hereby disclaims any responsibility for them.

Dedicated to my Grandchildren, Vincent and Mila

Scripture quotations are taken from the American Standard Version Bible (Public Domain).

Interior Image Credit: Diana Hastings
Editor: Pat Odabashian

ISBN: 978-1-6642-8582-8 (sc)
ISBN: 978-1-6642-8583-5 (e)

Library of Congress Control Number: 2022922611

Print information available on the last page.

WestBow Press rev. date: 12/12/2022

Psalm 119:35
Make me go into the path of thy commandments;
For therein do I delight. ASV

It's a cool cloudy fall day in Granmama's courtyard patio as the children eagerly sit at her feet ready to begin their dreamland journey. Their little eyes take in the delightful twinkling lights cascading all around the patio, wondrously entwining the plants. The children's delight makes her joy complete.

"Hello my precious children. Oh, what a wonderful dreamland journey we have planned for you," Granmama says lovingly. "I pray your day was filled with love, peace, joy and lots of laughter. Granmama is here."

Lifting her hand to Jesus, she says, "Let's kneel before the Lord in bedtime prayer. Dear Father, you are our hiding place. You keep us safe in your unending love. Hold us close and grant us a good night's sleep."

Looking at the little ones, she beckons them saying, "Children, let your request be known to the Lord."

They each silently pray to the Lord and peace fills their little faces. As they finish, Granmama continues, "We love and thank you Father, Son and Holy Spirit."

"Now close your eyes, get cuddly buggly and dig deep into your soft pillow. Take a deep breath in through your nose and slowly release it out of your mouth...1...2...3

Reaching for their hands, Granmama says, "Here, take hold of my hands as we enter our dreamland journey."

In the distance, Lulu and Vincent call out, "Granma, Granma! Over here! We're out in the courtyard waiting for you and the dreamland kids."

"Let's go children," Granmama says excitedly. "Let's go out to the courtyard to meet them."

"Hi, my darling children," she calls out with great delight as she sees Vincent and Lulu.

Lulu sits on the bench under the tree while Vincent has found a pile of fallen leaves to perch on.

"I should have known you'd choose the pile of leaves to the bench my beautiful boy," Granmama proclaims as he tosses up leaves everywhere and the children join him.

Vincent and Lulu chime in, "Hi Grams, Hi Kids. We love you all!"

"I'm super excited about our dreamland journey!" Vincent yells.

"I even wrote a song for us. It is especially for this dreamland journey. I hope everyone likes it."

"How wonderful," cries out Granmama, as the children gather close to Vincent. "I can't wait to hear it!"

"Grams!" shouts Vincent. "Tell them where we're going."

"Yes, yes, please do," agrees Lulu.

Granmama gently brushes away the leaves that cover Vincent from head to toe and sweetly announces, "We're going to a very special ice cream parlor."

"It's my ice cream parlor," Vincent blurts enthusiastically. "Vincent's Dream Freeze Ice Cream Parlor. I make and serve all the ice cream, just for you."

The children, unable to contain their excitement, jump, twirl and even flip as they cheer and laugh. In the distance, the sound of playful music and a tooting horn, catches their attention.

"Haaaa" Granmama laughs. "Now, this is a special surprise! Children, look down the courtyard; it's the cutest ice cream truck I've ever seen! It has an ice cream cone on top of it."

Suddenly, a whirring sound fills the air as helicopter blades spin around the top of the ice cream truck.

"Wait a minute!" exclaims Granmama. "It's a helicopter ice cream truck! How cool is that?"

The children run towards the truck with shrills of great delight!

"Oh Dreamland," Granmama sighs as she reflects, "You are always full of fun surprises."

"Come on everyone! Let's get on board!"," shouts Vincent. "Hey! Uncle Frank! Yay! And baby Mila, too! You two joined us again in our dreamland journey," he says as he reaches in for a big hug. "I love you both, forever!"

"We love you more!" responds Uncle Frank.

"Can you fly this helicopter ice cream truck?" asks Vincent

"In Dreamland, I can do just about anything," says Uncle Frank. "In this dreamland journey, I'm your pilot. Let's get ready to take off kids! Buckle up!"

"Frank, Mila, my beautiful baby girl," coos Granmama lovingly, "I'm so glad you joined us! Frank, you make a very handsome helicopter ice cream truck pilot!" Looking around she continues, "It's so spacious and comfy in here."

Suddenly, Vincent throws his arms up in the air and shouts, "It's countdown time! 5...4...3...2...1 Blast Off!"

The air is filled with cheers and laughter as the helicopter blades buzz and whirr and lift the ice cream truck into the cool fall sky.

"Hey kiddos!" announces Uncle Frank. "Look out the windows, we're flying over the Zoo."

"Hooray!" they all shout.

"Yay!" yells out Vincent. "I love all animals and all nature! I have a call of nature. Just call me the nature prayer warrior."

He then takes on a peaceful prayerful pose and with whispering lips, all the children join in.

"Oh, how cute!" exclaims Lulu. "I see a mommy gorilla and her baby reaching up to us."

"She took my hand!" exclaims Vincent. "They love us!"

"Wowee! The giraffes' necks are so long, they reach us way up here," says Granmama.

"Hi giraffe," giggles Mila as she reaches out to rub its nose. "I love your long neck."

"Look everyone! It's the lion's island. Oh, my goodness, they're black lions!" exclaims Vincent. "Kings of the jungle."

Of course, all the children start roaring and making their best lion faces.

To entertain the children, the black lions rear up on their hind legs and roar.

So thrilled, the children yell out, "Kings of the jungle!"

Granmama leans toward Uncle Frank and says, "I see big white fluffy clouds up ahead".

"Yep, could be a little bumpy, kiddos. Hold on tight and enjoy the rock n roll," Uncle Frank says as he sings out a rock n roll rhythm.

"Yipee!" the children cry out.

"This bumpy ride is fun!" shouts Vincent as he bangs on his air guitar. "Rock n roll!", he yells rocking out to the bumpy ride.

The children's joy and laughter fill the sky.

Lulu spots their destination and announces, "I see the ice cream parlor up ahead. It looks amazing! It has giant size ice cream cones on the roof."

Vincent chimes in, "And the trees around it are shaped like ice cream cones! That was baby Mila Bear's idea."

"It's so imaginative and fun!" remarks Granmama as she reaches for her grandchildren.

"Ok kiddos," reports Uncle Frank. "We're coming in for a landing. Hold on tight!"

Excitedly, the children hold onto each other tightly, giggling the whole way.

"We're here! Hooray!" shouts Vincent as he jumps up in the air.

"Ha, ha, ha," laughs Granmama. "This is so delightful! We've landed on the rooftop and are surrounded by adorable giant ice cream cones!"

"Let's have fun kiddos!" Frank sings out. "I'm ready for a Vincent's Dreamy Freeze Special!"

"Welcome to my Dream Freeze Ice Cream Parlor," Vincent yells out. "Follow me!"

Skipping, leaping and twirling, the children laugh and cheer as they follow him.

Calling the children's attention, to the exciting entrance into the parlor, Lulu states, "These giant ice cream cones are elevator vacuum pods that Vincent and Uncle Frank designed. Choose your favorite ice cream pod and jump in."

"It'll take you into the parlor," Vincent says, as he hops up on Uncle Frank's shoulders.

Everyone is awestruck by the adorable ice cream parlor.

"It's filled with darling bright colored ice cream lights," describes Granmama. "I see you all found your stools. They're so cushy and comfy."

"Press the colored buttons on the tabletop to create your own dream freeze. The table slides open, and your dream freeze comes out!" cheers Vincent. "But be ready to grab it! It's a fun challenge!"

"Oh Vincent, this really is so much fun! I caught my dream freeze," laughs Granmama. "Ha, ha, ha, it has two scoops! Strawberry cheesecake and chocolate mint chip. Yummy!"

"I made the ice cream myself," exclaims Vincent. "Well, Grams and Lulu helped, of course. I got my fav! Chunky monkey and orange dream freeze with a chocolate dipped cone covered in sprinkles!"

The dreamland children create the most delicious dream freezes ever and heartily eat them up!

"Uncle Frank, baby Mila and I are having the Vincent Dream Freeze Special," chuckles Lulu. "Frozen blue raspberry and frozen cherry cola with a rainbow cone."

"I must say, these dreamy freeze cones are very unique and delish!" remarks Granmama gratefully. "Good job my darling Vincent."

They lift Vincent high up in the air as they cheer and laugh.

"It's time to hear Vincent's special song that he wrote for our journey," Granmama says prayerfully. "But first, the dreamland children have stories about doing something kind for someone else that they want to share."

"Can I share my story?" asks Vera. "I love our dreamland journeys. They've taught me so much about Jesus and His love for us."

"Aw, that makes my heart happy. Yes, please share your story," replies Granmama.

My neighbors' fence was broken, so my mommy and I helped them fix and paint it," exclaims Vera.

"I didn't know work could be so much fun and how much love and joy I could feel in my heart helping others," she sighs with a heart full of gratitude.

"That's a wonderful story of the Lord's love in action, Vera. Thank you for sharing my darling," Granmama says. "Oliver, are you ready to share your story?"

"Yes, yes, yes!" he cries out. "I never miss a dreamland journey! I'm the number one fan!"

"Number one fan!" the gang cries out!

"The other day," he continues, "my mommy and I took a basket of food to our neighbors who didn't have enough food for their children."

"We played all afternoon and now we are best friends forever!"

"These stories make my heart happy, too," replies Vincent tearfully.

"My mommy and I took chickens to our neighborhood orphanage, so the kids have eggies for breakfast," sings out Adelyn, "and they invited us to eat with them."

"We sang praise songs and prayed together. It was the best day ever!"

"God's kingdom is righteousness, peace and joy. When we walk in the way of the Lord," explains Granmama, "loving, caring and helping others, it fills us with happiness, and our joy overflows. You darling children all felt love, joy and happiness in your hearts and I'm sure the families you helped felt the same way."

"Vincent, are you ready to share your song?"

The children roar out, "Vincent! Vincent!" and laugh out loud.

"Mommy!" cries out baby Mila, as she sees her mother coming through the door.

"Tia Marcela!" hollers Vincent.

They run into her arms with the dreamland children running right behind them.

"Hi, my darling Marcela," says Granmama as she joins the group hug. "Thank you for joining us and bringing the keyboard."

"I wouldn't miss this dreamland journey for anything! There's no other place I'd rather be!" answers Marcela.

"You're my hero!" responds Uncle Frank as he embraces his beautiful wife.

"Ok! Let's get this party started!"
Uncle Frank shouts excitedly as he and
baby Mila bear take their places at the
keyboard.

Together they play a lively duet for
Vincent's song.

Composing himself, Vincent sings his
special song.

"Jesus is my best friend

He is always with me

He teaches me the way of life

To love, care and help

To be all He created me to be.

He fills my heart with gladness

And overflowing joy

To share with all my dreamland friends

This makes me a happy boy!"

Together, everyone yells out, "best day EVER!"

"Yes," agrees Granmama, "best day ever!"

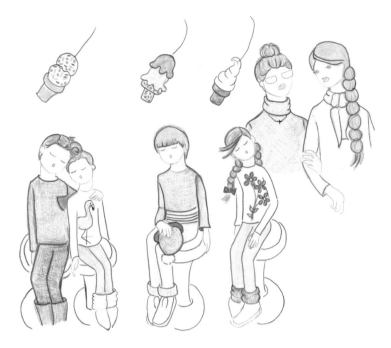

"Hmmm, did you feel that?" Granmama asks.

"Yes," answers Lulu. "The wind has shifted."

"Oh yes, I feel the shift in the wind. The children are on their stools ready to journey home," continues Granmama. "The parlor is gently swaying."

"The parlor stools are slowly spinning and drifting close together," Lulu says quietly.

"Hmm, Uncle Frank and his family are getting cuddly buggly for sleep time. I love them dearly," says Granmama.

"The stools are rocking back and forth," whispers Granmama.

"They are spinning and tilting, ever so gently, slipping the children carefully into their cozy beds."

Vincent and Lulu let out a big yawn and sigh, "Best day ever Granmama! Good night dreamland friends, we love you all!"

"Good night my sweet children," Granmama whispers.

Day is done

Night has begun

Hush and rest my little ones

I pray we may be one

In the Spirit, Father and the Son.

Printed in the United States
by Baker & Taylor Publisher Services